reaching for sun

reaching for sun

Tracie Vaughn Zimmer

Published by Bloomsbury U.S.A Children's Books
175 Fifth Avenue, New York, NY 10010
Distributed to the trade by Holtzbrinck Publishers

Library of Congress Cataloging-in-Publication Data
Zimmer, Tracie Vaughn.
Reaching for sun / by Tracie Vaughn Zimmer. — 1st U.S. ed.
p.   cm.
Summary: Josie, who lives with her mother and grandmother and has cerebral palsy,
befriends a boy who moves into one of the rich houses behind her old farmhouse.
ISBN-13: 978-1-59990-037-7 • ISBN-10: 1-59990-037-8
[1. Cerebral palsy—Fiction. 2. People with disabilities—Fiction. 3. Friendship—
Fiction. 4. Grandmothers—Fiction. 5. Single-parent families—Fiction. 6. Novels in
verse.] I. Title.
PZ7.5.Z63Re 2007   [Fic]—dc22   2006013197

First U.S. Edition 2007
Designed and typeset by Nicole Gastonguay
Flower illustrations by Shadra Strickland
Printed in the U.S.A. by Quebecor World Fairfield
10 9 8 7 6 5 4

For my mother,
Pauline Courtney Schwitalski,
and in memory of my grandmothers,
Jane Wyatt Stines,
Ollie DePew Vaughn, and
Lenora "Jackie" Whittington Courtney

reaching for sun

winter

Then let not winter's ragged hand deface
In thee thy summer.

—William Shakespeare (SONNET VI)

not even me

The late bell rings,
but
I'm hiding
in the last stall
of the girls' bathroom
until I hear
voices
disappear behind closing
classroom doors.

Only then
do I slip out
into the deserted hallway
and rush to room 204,
a door
no one
wants to be seen opening.

Not even
me.

tomatoes

With my odd walk
and slow speech
everyone knows
I've got special ed,
but if I wait
until the hall clears,

taunts like tomatoes
don't splatter
the back of my head.

break

It's the last day
before winter break,
when the hallway is littered with
Christmas ribbons and wrappings,
when presents are passed
between romances and friends.

As I walk through the door
Mrs. Sternberg hands me
a lunch bag
decorated with stickers and stamps
that's full of candy,
but it won't change
the lonely taste
of seventh grade.

invisible

If being assigned to room 204
wasn't bad enough,
now the new occupational therapist
(Mrs. Swaim)
appears to escort me
to her torture chamber.

She nags me
(just like Mom)
about wearing my splint.

She reminds me
(just like Mom)
to do the painful stretches
and exercises.

But my thumb will always be pasted to my palm,
and my left wrist and shoulder
connected
by an invisible rubber band
called cerebral palsy.

the bus

I sit third row on the bus,
try to scrunch myself
tight
against the frosted window,
feet on fire
from the heater beneath.

Hiding—again—
from this week's troublemakers
assigned
to the first row:
Natalie Jackson, for cussing;
Pete Yancey, for spitwads;
Caleb Harrison, for flipping off
a delivery guy.
And from their friends who sit
in the back of the bus—
caged animals waiting to be unleashed
in the Falling Waters neighborhood.

I'm last to get released
from this rolling tortured tin can,
as they head off in pairs and packs—
joking,
laughing,
gossiping,
planning,
new scenes
for their perfect lives.

home

In the kitchen
Gran's stationed at her double oven,
four pots
bubbling and steaming,
sweat beading on her upper lip.
Her friend Edna (the complainer)
stands near the sink
mixing a giant bowl of batter.

"Hi, Ms. Edna."

"Hello, honey."

"How was school, Josie-bug?" Gran asks,
wiping her face with her oven-mitted hand.

"Okay," I lie—
in front of her friend.

Edna hands off a wooden spoon
for me to stir
the caramel on the double boiler—
the main ingredient for Gran's famous
popcorn balls.

Already coconut bars,
divinity (little white flowers
that melt on your tongue),
and vanilla fudge march across countertops
on wax paper.

We'll deliver them all to Lazy Acres,
the nursing home
where Gran visits her "old" friends.

The one place
other than here
only smiles greet me.

uniform

Each day
Gran wears
khaki elastic pants,
a crisp white collared shirt
that never gets spotted
no matter how much
she cooks
or works in the garden.

Her brown vinyl purse
is always within reach,
and she'll unearth almost anything
from its secret compartments.

Her long hair
stays fastened in a bun
with chopsticks
until bedtime,
when it waterfalls
down near to her waist.

She grew up
in this very house,
the only daughter after four sons
and the single one
to survive
and inherit the farm—

though now
there's only five acres
left of it
to call her own.

double major

Ten minutes after Edna leaves
Mom flies through the front door
from her job waiting tables
at the Lunchbox Café
next to the Ford plant.

She pecks Gran on the cheek,
me on the head,
but never stops moving
or talking the whole time.

Grabs her lunch bag
(and two pieces of fudge),
changes out of her yellow polyester uniform,
and heads straight out the back door
in a run—

and that's all I'll see her today.

She's got finals this week,
and then one semester left
at the community college
with a double major
in business administration
and landscape design.

So she's just a blip
on the screen
of my life
these days.

drop out

I don't know much
about my father except
he was a freshman in college
just like Mom
when I was conceived—
though he didn't drop out on *his* dreams.

I wonder
if he ditched me and Mom
when he found out about my disability,
or if it gave him the excuse he needed—
typed letter left behind in the mailbox,
no stamp.

I wonder
if I got my straight
blond hair, blue eyes,
and cowardice from him,
and whether he's real smart,
rich, and now got himself
a picture-perfect family.

I wonder whether
he likes pepper on his
corn on the cob like me,
or poetry
before slipping off to sleep.
When I asked Mom
she always answered:
"I don't know,"
between her teeth
until I stopped asking.

Gran said she knew
next to nothing about him
and thought of him even less.

If we met one day
accidentally,
say, in an airport,
I wonder
if he'd be carrying
my baby picture
behind his license.

I wonder
if I could forgive him—
let myself be folded
into his warm embrace,
or if
I'd spit on that picture
and scratch out my
face so he couldn't pretend
to care about me anymore.

fingertip pieces of dreams

Gran stretches to store
her rose-covered shoe box
back up in the hall closet.
You'd think she taught
first grade,
not just Sunday school,
the way she loves
cutting and pasting her way
through winter.
She snips out pictures of
fences, flowers, plants, and pots
from seed catalogs and
gardening magazines—
a puzzle of her dream spring garden
with no perfect fit.
Just as she tips the box into place,
it falls.

Out flutter
petals of color

and Granny lands
on her wide bottom.
I rush to her side,
help her find her balance.
It takes half an hour
to carefully pick up these
fingertip pieces of dreams
and click the heavy closet door
on them again.

aunt laura

My mom's best friend,
Aunt Laura
(though she's not really my aunt),
visits each December
with her son, Nathan,
who's also in seventh grade.

Mom and Aunt Laura
shop for days on end
while Nathan and I
watch movies
or play checkers—
silently.

Mom and Aunt Laura
stay up almost until dawn
never running out of words.
Nathan and I
ice cookies
while Granny sings off-key

to her vinyl
holiday albums.

After spending days
leading to Christmas
together each year,
you'd think
Nathan and I
would be friends—

but we're
not.

gifts

It's a tradition
that we only get three gifts
each year—

"Was enough for Jesus," Gran says—
and two of them must be homemade.

Gran taught me to crochet
with my good hand,
and we figured out a way
to make the yarn
loop around the frozen
fingers on my left.

It's taken three months
to make them each
a wooly scarf
and mittens
in their favorite colors—
purple for mom
and fuchsia for Gran.

Next year it might take me
six months,
but I'm going to learn how to knit!

holiday buffet

On Christmas Eve
we buy up the gala apples
with thumbprint bruises,
oranges, scaly and puckered,
even bananas spotted like
Granny's hands.
Cutting the fruit into wedges,
and then piercing them with large paper clips.
Stringing popcorn,
raisins, and cereal
until the tips of our fingers ache.

Huge pinecones
get smeared with peanut butter
sent from Aunt Laura's
down in North Carolina,
then sprinkled with sunflower seeds
and bird feed until they're coated.
We dress our white pine tree
just outside

the family room window
with these offerings.
Then kill the lights
and watch
the holiday feast.

midnight service

At midnight
we bundle into the
darkened church.

Kids from school
who usually pretend I'm invisible
wish me Merry Christmas
and say hello
in front of their parents.

But the hymns
I can't even sing
warm and light me
like the small white candle
flickering
in my good hand.

holiday

On Christmas
we stay in pajamas—
all day—

nibble the ham
Gran baked
between homemade biscuits
Mom can create from scratch
in fourteen minutes flat.

We watch
old movies
(though all our hands fiddle on projects
the whole time)
or work on a new five-thousand-piece puzzle
that won't get swept off the dining room table
until we finish it
just before Thanksgiving.

These few days:
the best ones
of the year.

presents

Mom's so surprised
over her scarf and gloves—
didn't even know
I could crochet
since she hasn't been home
most of the fall.

Gran's scarf is a little uneven,
but she doesn't seem
to mind.

Mom painted each pot
for Gran's ever-increasing collection of violets—
and gave her a gift certificate for seeds
from an heirloom vegetable catalog.

Gran created a quilted book bag for Mom
and a robe soft as a puppy.

I love
the blue jeans jacket Mom bought
and beaded.
Gran embroidered
a journal with my initials
and unveiled a new quilt for my bed
in the colors of summer—

watermelon, tomato, blue skies,
and lemonade.

the back acre

Christmas afternoon we pull boots
over our pajamas, bundle up,
and hike the snowless landscape
to the back acre,
where most of the family is buried
inside the wrought-iron fence
under an ancient hemlock tree.

Four generations of Wyatts
owned this land
before Gran—
near to a thousand acres.

When Papaw died,
Gran ran it for several years
best she knew how
renting out acres to farmers,
canning any vegetable she could.

But when Mom wanted college
more than a farm,

and my medical bills
stacked up on the dining room table,
Gran resigned herself to sell it to her friend.

At first the farmer
who bought it didn't change a thing,
but when Mr. Killick got sick too,
his kids put him in Lazy Acres and sold
all of it to the developer that built
the mansions up behind us.

Gran places silk poinsettias on top
of each Wyatt stone.
"My momma would understand what I had to do,"
Gran says,
"but I'll have to answer
to Daddy one day."
Then she turns her face
into the wind
and walks away.

clothes

There's more new clothes
on the first day back
from Christmas break
than the first day of school;
no one wanting to look
eager in September.

I may stick out
in every other way
in the hallways of middle school,
but my outfits
can compete
even with the rich kids
from the neighborhood behind us.

Mom might pester me
about homework
and my exercises and therapies,
but on fashion
we always agree.

the table

I hate
the mosaic-topped kitchen table
Mom created,
not because it wobbles,
or the food that's served on it
(the best part, by far),
but because it's her favorite
place to pounce.

Mom plops across from me
at breakfast,
and even though it's Saturday
and school just got started again,
she forces me to review
a giant stack of flash cards
for the end-of-year tests.

Then a list
of exercises she's gotten
from the speech therapist,

occupational therapist,
and physical therapist.

I think tomorrow
I'll skip breakfast.

january

The only good thing
about January?

Halfway to June.

spring

Even the pine trees
Appear new
In spring.

—Izumi Shikibu

kingdom of imaginary worlds

An oily stink
blows in again from the bulldozers—
those metal monster dinosaurs
that scar the landscape
behind our old farm.
The tornadoes of dust they kick up
as they move closer each season
leave the porch cushions
and our teeth
dusted with a grimy film.
The echoes
of early-morning hammering
wake me
even on Saturday mornings.
And though I hate
what they've done
to my kingdom of imaginary worlds—
fairy towns and factories
closed,
the summer camp for ogres

shut down,
a homeless shelter for gnomes
flattened—
with chin on knees
I can't help but study the men,
busy as bugs,
not satisfied until they
block another tree
from me.

poppies

When poppies first
push themselves
out of the ground
they look like a weed—
hairy, grayish, saw-toothed foliage—
easily a member
of the ugly family.

When I push
sounds from my mouth
it's not elegant either.
I wrestle to wrap
my lips
around syllables,
struggle with my tongue
to press the right points.

When poppies bloom
the same red
as a Chinese wedding dress—

satiny cups with ruffled edges,
purplish black eyes—
they're a prize for patience,
and if I take all that trouble
to say something,
I promise
to try
to make it worth
the wait too.

despite

Mom and I lug
house plants
back outside
from Granny's rusting metal plant stand
that's blocking our one picture window
so you can never tell
who's pulling in the drive
through the tangle of green.

Just like the plants,
I dream of being
back outside for long summer days,
not stuck
in occupational therapy
twice a week,
speech therapy three times a week,
or tortured at the kitchen table
with flash cards
the little time Mom spends at home.

Mom wants me
to love school like she does,
follow her lead to college,
make my mark:
the first astronaut with
cerebral palsy,
or at least
a doctor or lawyer,
something with a title or abbreviations, I guess.
But Mom's dreams for me
are a heavy wool coat I
wear, even in summer.

backyard archaeology

I'm using the hand spade to plant
zinnias Granny started weeks ago
when I unearth a whole peanut shell
in the dark soil.
Gran's told the story
dozens of times—
how in the 1920s the nasty boll weevil
nearly stole the note to this farm.
Gran's two oldest brothers went off
to the factories in the north
to keep paying the taxes
while the little ones tried
to pick the plants clean
of the nasty devils. Hopeless.

So Great-Grandpa turned to peanuts.
One of the first to try the new crop—
a rare old bird, he was, too—
believing King Cotton could be overthrown
by a beetle.

Still, he saved this farm
when most around these
parts were lost.

But now
his big dreams, all lost,
empty
as the shell in my hand.

dress of leaves

I'm hidden
beneath the willow tree,
spying out her dress of leaves,
counting the roofers
on the latest house
that grows
behind us.

Suddenly
the dark parts.
A wedge of light and a boy
slip through,
the air sucked from my lungs
like a vacuum.

The boy's face freezes like stone.
I cough uncontrollably.

"Sorry. I was following
a *Danaus plexippus*

and thought it flew in here."
When I try to speak
my voice is on vacation
and a high-pitched squeak
comes out instead.

"I didn't mean to scare you . . ."
he says,
backing out.

"No. It's okay,"
I finally stammer.
"Is it a bird?"

"No. A monarch butterfly."

"Oh!"
My voice like new chalk,
but surprised by my bravery,
"Come on. I know
where they'll be."

"You do?"

"Sure—on *Buddleia*,
butterfly bush."
And that's how I meet Jordan,
the boy who just moved
into the rich neighborhood
that keeps spreading
behind us.

searching

I follow Jordan
as he examines leaves
from plants,
looks for insects on their undersides.

He pulls out his plant guidebook
to search for names
I already know.

"How do you know the name
of every plant?"

I shrug. "Always have."

Jordan catches an inchworm,
puts it on my palm.
We watch it fold itself
again and again
up my arm
to my smiling face.

leapfrog

On the east side of the house
is Gran's formal garden.
She always meant to visit
France or England,
but never got the chance
or the money.
Widowed at twenty-five and
working at the paper factory
didn't buy plane tickets,
and raising a girl by yourself
was hard enough without dreams
of your own.
So she planted rows of boxwoods
in diamonds and rectangles,
lined the paths with crushed bricks
that crunch as you walk along.
Then planted Grace Darling teacup roses
and placed a wrought-iron
patio table in the center
of the shapes.

When Granny serves Jordan and me
Earl Grey tea
and butter cookies
but insists we call them biscuits,
Jordan doesn't even roll his eyes—
and my heart leapfrogs
with the word
"friend."

an acre of imagination

Jordan's yard (and all his neighbors', too)
is so serious:
lawn buzzed down like
a Marine recruit's cut
and each house has:
two terra-cotta pots
perfectly placed on the porch—
color-coordinated bouquets
(like purses and shoes that
grannies and little girls wear
for Easter Sunday)
that match the front door—
and nothing more.

Our house is a crazy quilt of color
pots of every shape and size
nestled everywhere—
some hand painted,
others mortared with mismatched
chipped china,

all bursting with at least
three different plants—
sweet potato vine,
caladium,
lamb's ear—
Gran's palette
of color and texture.

The old shed
wears a half-done mural of the Eiffel Tower
made out of broken glass
and the sun dances across it
each day.

Baskets get tucked into
elbows of tree limbs,
window boxes painted navy blue
to show off the tuberous begonias spilling out
against the peeling gray clapboards.
Even our mailbox chokes
with a tangle of vermillion trumpet vines.

Our new neighbors
might call this a hillbilly's cottage
and find our mix of colors
unfashionable.

But Gran says when she sold off
all but a slice of this old farm
she didn't sell
the imagination of the Wyatt women with it,
though I wonder
if we could bleach it—
just a bit.

me, the dandelion

Gran calls Jordan's dad at work
so he can go with us.
His dad says from now on we don't
even have to ask.
We pile into her Jeep filled with
two-inch starter pots—
off to Lazy Acres,
where we help hands knotted
like asparagus fern roots
remember the feel of soil and spring.

It's the only place
where I don't stick out
like a dandelion
in a purple petunia patch,
and I like Jordan seeing me
in a place I belong—
everybody's granddaughter.

I dream of the lives
my hands
might know,
like all of those
I help here.

small envelopes

Today, the most popular girl in seventh grade,
Natalie Jackson,
slipped invitations between the vents in lockers,
passed them across my desk in algebra,
dropped them in laps as she glided
back to her throne
in the last row on the bus.

But this time
I didn't have to study tornado drill directions
in the cafeteria
or pretend interest in the road signs,
because Jordan
filled that ever-vacant seat at the table
and then the canyon of green vinyl on the bus too,
then skipped his own stop and followed me on
home
like a stray.

stuck to my tongue

Each year
since I could walk
Granny's built me
a hiding place.
But I'm embarrassed to see her
poking the bamboo poles in the ground,
tied at the top like a teepee
with leftover yarn.
She'll plant them with scarlet runner beans
that will curl and dangle,
twisting their way
to the top—
shading my secret spot.

I wish she'd realize
I'm really much too old
for one now,
but the words get stuck
to my tongue
each time
I try to tell her.

autograph

Granny cuts orange yarn for us—
left over from lap quilts
she crochets
for the folks at Lazy Acres.
We loop the yarn in the plot Gran tilled today,
stepping back
to check our work—
even once from my window upstairs.
Finally, we slit open the bank envelope—
the marigold seeds' winter home—
and we drip them
along the orange lines
in the cool dark soil
and dream of our signatures
blooming by summer:
Josie and Jordan.

whirligigs

Jordan knows
odd facts
about everything,
like how a day on Saturn is ten hours long
or how many people rode the first Ferris wheel (2,160).

But each day Jordan reminds the other seventh graders
that this kid who is a whole year younger than them
knows so much more—
it makes him about as popular as a pop quiz.
And even though he lives in the largest
of the brick mansions behind us
(where most of the well-liked rich kids live)
his house looks like the moving truck
just pulled away.
No pictures on the walls,
dusty boxes still stacked
in the corners of rooms,
no curtains
on any of the windows.
It even smells empty.

I learn Jordan's mom died in an accident
when he was just a toddler,
and his dad really is
a rocket scientist
who works seventy hours each week.
So Jordan never had a shot to learn
some of the basics:
Don't correct a teacher in front of her class
or launch up your hand with every answer.
He stands a little too close,
and his catalog clothes
might cost a bunch,
but they don't match much.

His brown curly hair
drapes over dark chocolate eyes
and when he smiles, all his teeth
and even some gum
show besides.

He's always excited
about some new experiment
to try in the garden
or at the lab in his
new basement.

But I've learned this fact for myself:
Days spin faster than a whirligig
in a spring storm
by the side
of my new friend.

bus stop

The path to the creek
isn't too far,
and the bridge
Grandpa built
when Mom was just a baby
still solid as stone—
six doors down from that is Jordan's house.
Each morning now
Jordan shows up on our screened-in porch,
munching from a baggie of cereal
before I even have my shoes on.

After school,
Mr. DeLong, the bus driver,
makes him get off in his own neighborhood,
but he's waiting on our screened porch
by the time I get home.

jewels

The golden bushes out front
called forsythia are blooming now—
their long arms
trying to waltz with wind.
Granny, Jordan, and I cut
their dance short,
arrange them
in colored glass vases for
Gran's old friends at Lazy Acres.
We turn the leftovers into
bracelets, crowns, necklaces:

jewels
that wilt by afternoon.

flicker

We go
to Jordan's house
to pick up beakers, his microscope,
and graph paper
to set up another experiment
(this one measuring spores
on different kinds of ferns).
The foyer echoes
like the gym at school,
and it feels like nobody lives here
and almost,
they don't.

A maid cleans.
A crew cuts the lawn.
Even the groceries get delivered.
Jordan's dad is home, for once,
but he barely lifts his head
from his laptop to meet me.

His eyes
flicker in surprise,
but he slams
his attention back to the screen
and coughs to dismiss us.

In ten minutes we fill a big box,
and I don't see the inside
of Jordan's house
again for months.

snake

Between bites of PB and J
Jordan is telling me
about poisonous snakes
when
Natalie Jackson and her followers
arrive like royalty
a few seats down
in the cafeteria.

They start teasing us
about being in love—
the genius and the 'tard.

My throat feels like
I've swallowed an orange
whole.

But Jordan
goes on and on
(though the tips of his ears turn
crimson),

even repeats himself some,
about the preferred habitats of each species,
how you're really not
supposed to suck out the venom
like in the movies,
and how they keep the rat population
in check.

Finally, Natalie and her tribe
leave to dump their trays, find fresh prey.

"You never know when you
might run into a snake,"
Jordan repeats.

"That's true," I agree,
as we watch some slither
on past.

snoring

Afternoons
you can always find Granny
reading a gardening magazine
or at least find one
blanketing her chest
as she snores
in her hammock
stretched over the unfurling face of hosta
and fingers of ferns.
The old
sycamores out back
create dollops of shade.

You can find Mom
(if she's home)
slumped over the landscape designs
(her final semester project),
long runner's legs
forever twitching or swinging—
the woman never sits still.

Now you can find me
with Jordan,
parked in the garden
building a trap for insects
or graphing the growth on our marigold plants
or just watching the day yawn,
noting in my notebook
all the changes I see.

the question

We're building
a tadpole fort
complete with fresh water
dipped from the creek
and beta food from the pet store
when Jordan asks
(like no one else will):

"You have cerebral palsy, don't you?"

Surprised, I only nod.

"Were you born with it?"

I nod again.

"How does it happen?"

"A vein pops in the brain
and ruins the parts
where it spills."

He nets up a tadpole,
measures it,
and writes down the data.
"What's the hardest part?"

I don't hesitate:
"Everyone thinking I'm retarded."

"But Josie,
you know tons of stuff! Anybody
who talks to you knows that."

But at school,
only Jordan knows.

three feet square

One of the four
experiments
Jordan and I have running
in the garden
is a patch of dirt
three feet square.
Nothing much interesting about it—
a mint plant,
some scraggly Russian sage,
and three peonies with ants
always exploring the velvety pink blooms.
Once a week
we study this one plot of land,
count the insects,
describe and graph the changes in the plants,
take a picture for a time line too.
Jordan's taught me
not to glance
but to *look*,
even study,

the complicated lace of a web,
the frilly holes from beetle snacks,
the dew like diamond earrings on the tips of leaves—
finding miniature miracles
I was once blind to.

kiss of life

Finally, for Mother's Day,
we get Granny a gift that's not
"too good to use"
(new slippers remain wrapped
in tissue paper in the top of her closet
with all our other good ideas).

We got her a pump
since the old well has been dry
for a year now.

She casts that twenty-pound pump
in the creek
like a left-handed pitcher
in a Little League game.

Gran will stand like a preacher
over her hollyhock, columbine, lady's mantle,
and coneflower,

humming hymns to them
with her wand of water,
baptizing each bed
with the kiss of life.

wildflower mix

Summer's not far away—
I dream of
sleeping in late
with no nagging from Mom
for ten whole weeks.

But without asking,
Mom registered me
for a summer clinic
so speech and occupational therapists
can test their latest methods
on me.

But I'm sick of spending
all my time
working on what's wrong
with me.
I don't want to be
pruned or pinched back
like a wilting petunia.

I want this summer
to be a wildflower-seed mix.
And me, surprised
by what blooms.

like me

The bulldozers
are at it again,
ripping out more trees
as they come closer each season.
And my favorite:
an enormous elm
who held the sun's golden face
in her arms the whole day.

But this spring
half the branches wear no leaves,
claimed by disease or insects.
So the bulldozers
tear it from the soil
with their terrible teeth
and splatter the leaves and limbs
like garbage.

Why can't they see
that half still blooms—
like me?

summer

To see the Summer Sky
Is Poetry, though never in a Book it lie—
True Poems flee—

—Emily Dickinson

never

Mom's making me help her
cut the last blooming iris,
the first daisies.
Our tools talk to each other
though our lips are silent.
Jordan stops over, and she puts
him to work too.

We take the flowers on over to
the folks at Lazy Acres
nobody else goes to see.

Impatient
with Elma's long, wandering story,
Mom's leg under the table
sways like a metronome.
Her thoughts, I bet,
back in her books
about running a landscape center,
that half-baked attention

I recognize while she
tries to wait for my words too.

Then, she's back—
remembering to ask Mr. Howard
about his sick grandson,
comes round beside him,
pats his leathery brown hand—
listens to him
like her favorite song.

Jordan plops next to me
on the worn pink couch.
His face smeared with an awkward smile,
like he sewed it on at the door.
He squeezes my knee
with his sweaty hand
and it throbs, like a heartbeat,
under his touch
and though I'm sure he's ready to go
I never want to move.

note

It's the last day of school—
lockers stand open, bare.
The floor is piled with graded papers,
book reports,
ripped folders everywhere.
The teachers wear easy smiles.

In between room 204
and language arts,
I meet Jordan at my locker.
I hand him
the first note I ever wrote
a friend.

In it I tell him about
that clinic
Mom signed me up for
and ask him what I should do.

The next class takes forever
and my hands sweat
and my heart feels like a million monarchs
are inside it,
waiting for his words.

I open my locker
to find his one-sentence response:

Tell her you don't want to go.

As if she would listen
to me.

cold strands of spaghetti

Gran hands me a gigantic
philodendron,
vines so long they wind
around the top of the kitchen cabinets,
then hit the floor.
"Tell me," she says, "what you see."

"It needs water."

"How do you know?"

"The leaves, they're droopy."

"What else?"

"Some of the leaves are yellow; it might need a feeding."

"Yes. Now ease it out of that pot."

When I do, I see the roots are knotted
like cold strands of spaghetti.

"What does that mean, Josie?"

"It needs more room to grow."

"Exactly. That plant tells us exactly
how it wants to be treated.
You might learn something
from a philodendron."

graduation

Today is Mom's graduation
from Tidewater Community College
with her associate's in business
and landscape design.
She's the first ever
in our family
to get a degree.

Gran dropped out
in eighth grade to help on the farm
when her brothers got called up
for the war.
When they never came back
Gran gave up her dream
of being a stewardess—
and traveling all over the world.

But someday
I'll buy us a flight to France
and we'll sit under the Eiffel Tower
sharing a croissant.

daydreamer

In the box of summer clothes
I find
the scrapbook I made
last summer:
tickets I created to places I've never been,
letters to friends that never existed,
pressed flowers from the garden.

I'm daydreaming about how different
this summer can be
when Jordan finds me—
so excited his voice snaps like a twig—
about a science camp
that lasts four weeks this summer.
"Besides," he says, "you'll be in that clinic
anyway."

A slap of words across my face.

the red plate

If you get good grades,
or graduate,
land a new job,
or just any small thing,
Gran will fix your favorite meal
and serve you on our
one red plate.

Mom's had it twice this month
already,
and now with her new job
at the landscape center in town
I guess it'll be nasty
liver and onions again.

I'm craving my favorite—
breakfast for dinner,
Gran's biscuits and gravy.
But I can't think of a way
to earn it
yet.

ripples of sunlight

Mom surprises Granny and me
with a weekend getaway
to celebrate the start of summer,
our first-ever vacation.
But best of all—
she invites Jordan!
The three-room cabin
is built on stilts and it feels
like a tree house
hidden in leaves.

The campground has mini golf,
movies out under the stars,
and a lake!
Granny wears her goofy
polka-dotted bathing suit
with the frilly skirt;
her wide hips
slip out the side like bread dough
rising in a pan.

She doesn't seem to care—
floats on top of the lake
like she owns the whole place.

Mom's turquoise bikini
flaunts her taut muscles
and sculpted thighs.
Her red hair fans out
like a peacock behind her.

Jordan is pasty white
in his black swimming trunks;
his shoulders look like the nub
of new growth on a tree.
In my swimsuit I feel exposed——
a seedling in a late frost.
My bony limbs all akimbo,
gaps in my purple suit instead of curves
like all the other girls
seem to have,
but my body nearly obeys me in water.

Jordan notices my freedom
though he doesn't seem to see the rest,
and we dunk each other
and chase,
his warm hands on my goose-fleshed
arms;
for the first time
someone touches me
like I won't shatter under their fingers.
Ripples of sunlight
spill in my veins,
and I wish
just this once
I could stop time.

maybe just a little

We take an afternoon to visit Monticello.
Mom and Jordan
share the pamphlet
about Jefferson's garden,
their shadows blending, two trees.

They talk in their
scientific geek code—
genus, phylum, species.
Mom even throws her arm
around his shoulders;
he looks up at her
like *she* invented
Jefferson's cannonball clock
we saw in the foyer of his famous home.

It makes me sick,
and maybe just a little jealous.
Jordan must wish
my mom was his,

and maybe she dreams
she'd given birth
to the perfect little genius.

I must be a real disappointment—
stunted foliage,
no yield.

cricket lullabies

In the car
Jordan taught me
Morse code.
Now at night,
through the thin pine boards
between our bunks,
we tap out messages
to each other.

My words finally able
to keep up with thoughts
off a page.

I decide
there's no way I'm going
to summer school
no matter what
Mom thinks—
I'm spending every second with Jordan
before he leaves.

Crickets sing their lullabies
to us,
and before dawn stretches
her arms into a new day
sleep tucks me in.

suit yourself

Gran and Jordan
decide to canoe across
the small campground lake.
They ask me to come,
but since I can't paddle,
I'd be stuck down
in the middle
like some baby.

I refuse.
Granny shrugs.
"Suit yourself."
They finally find a life jacket
that fits Granny's ample apple shape.
The red boat
slices the still waters like a knife;
something Jordan says makes Gran throw
her head like a horse
and laugh so it echoes.
I watch the water drip from the tips

of their oars,
diamond necklaces in the sun.

The urge to stomp my feet,
bite somebody,
scream:
He's *my* friend.
I'm not supposed to be
left out
anymore.

cutting

First real day of summer
and Mom is prodding me
with her "get out of bed" speech:
"We need to leave in twelve minutes."
"You must eat *something*."
"Are you wearing *that*?"
Yawn.

She's been like a Chihuahua with
a new toy since she landed that job.
And she's working hours
that would do Jordan's dad proud.

I don't speak to her,
I'm so angry over this.
But she doesn't even notice.

"I'll walk you in today,"
she says,
like it's preschool
registration.

It's worse
than I even imagined—
I'm the oldest one there, by far.
After a painful session of OT,
and speech when I'm paired with a fourth grader,
I walk out during a break
and head to Jordan's house.

omission

I tap on Jordan's back door;
he's watching cartoons and eating
marshmallow cereal straight out of the box.
When he asks if the clinic was canceled,
I just shrug
and grab a handful of cereal.
Then he's on to the chemicals
we'll need to change
the hydrangeas from pink to blue,
and wondering if with new mixtures
we could create our own colored
blooms.

When we arrive in the garden
Granny questions how I'm home so soon.
"It lets out early," I lie
and walk away,
hoping these few days with Jordan
before he leaves for camp are worth
the bitter taste on my tongue.

liar

For the last three days
when Mom drops me off
at the clinic
I walk through the front
and straight out the back
until I get to Jordan's door.

I tell Mom
the clinic's not so bad.
I tell Jordan and Gran
it's over early.
And it is—
for me anyway.

messages

At home,
I hover near the phone
to answer questions from the clinic
or erase ones that are left
while Gran lingers in the garden.
Each day I race
to check the mail for any letters
with that return address.
I hop on the phone
whenever it rings
though I've always hated to answer it.

Each day
my simple plan
gets more and more
complicated.

i can't name

Mom and I
hit the mall to buy Jordan's birthday present
(a potato electricity kit)
when we run into him and his dad
shopping for his clothes and camp supplies.

Somehow Mom ends up with
a wad of cash from Jordan's dad
(who heads back to the office, relieved,
and with an invitation for dinner and cake).
We spend the afternoon
under the fluorescent glow of the mall
helping Jordan shed
his gifted-boy-geek look—
new haircut and clothes.

Waiting outside the dressing room,
I nearly confess that I've been skipping
the clinic to Mom.
When I open my mouth to tell her,

Jordan walks out.
I see the words disappear
like a hummingbird
between racks of clothes.

He looks so different:
in athletic jerseys,
jean shorts pushed low,
and cool basketball shoes
that replace his hideous loafers.

When we walk through
the front door,
we see Gran hunched
over the flour-covered table,
rolling out dough,
cutting it into strips to drop
in the bubbly buttery broth.
Jordan's favorite meal:
chicken and dumplings,
and the sweet smell of
baking chocolate cake

to celebrate his
twelfth birthday.

Later, as we all
sing to him,
the candles light up his dark eyes
and a small flame
of something I can't name
sparks just beneath my heart.

daring the rain

Dark clouds roll in from the southwest,
ruining a perfect morning.
Blowing hate, she comes
throwing branches in
our tomato and corn rows,
thunder laughing while
crushing our work.
Leaves scatter like confetti
on this party of destruction.
Jordan and I
watch from the covered porch.
Saplings bow to her power,
the leaves of hosta
by the back stoop
throb
like a heartbeat.

Granny braced by the screen door,
fists on her wide hips,
surveying the sky,

daring the rain to
mist her face
with each gust.
Gran always says
"This tantrum can't last—
but we Wyatt women will."

swallow a frog

Jordan, Gran, and I are out in the garden
cleaning up debris but
Gran's face is etched with anger
and determination.
I know she has more on her mind
than just this storm.
Gran feels more like my mom
since Mom was always
busy with part-time jobs
and full-time college.
I can judge Granny's face faster than anything,
so I'm thinking it's a good time to
find an escape.
Before I can, she starts:
"You see this mess, Josie?
Well, your lies are going to cause one just
as costly, and not near so easy to clean up.
Tell your mom you've been skipping tonight—
or I'm going to do it for you."

Her eyes are squinted up
and her jaw is slack,
a portrait of disappointment.
Jordan looks like he swallowed a frog.
They both head into the house
and leave me holding
my rusty bucket. The yellow sky casts
an eerie glow of things to come.

god-sized broom

I find Jordan stretched out
in the hammock.
Last summer, I tried it once:
tangled for hours,
frightened and helpless,
like a spider's dinner.
He holds out his hand, helps
me scootch in.

The silence settles;
it's the perfect kind—
when you don't have to pretend
to know what to say.
His left arm and leg
warming my right.
For a long time
we watch
the clouds;
they look like they're
being swept
by a God-sized broom.

He turns his face
to mine
so close, then says:
"If I had a mom,
I wouldn't lie to her."

Then he climbs out,
disappears between
the soft green arms
of the forsythia
for the rest of the day.

discovery

When Mom takes off
to meet Aunt Laura in Raleigh
I discover something
I'd rather not know:
it's even easier to lie
to your mom
on the phone.

a good crop

Jordan leaves in forty-eight hours
and then I'll be stuck
alone again all summer.

And worse than that,
it feels like that
old boll weevil is back
on the farm
eating my insides—
feasting on lies.

invitation

Just before noon on Saturday,
only hours before Jordan leaves for camp,
I pack up my pride to find
him sitting on his front stoop
with a few test tubes
and some icky greenish liquid.
He tells me about his quest
for a new algae as if nothing
happened between us the other day.
Relieved, I park myself beside him.
Then Natalie appears around the redbrick garage
like a goddess,
lime bikini curving in all the right spots.
"Hey, we're playing water volley. Want to come?"
Natalie doesn't even glance my way.

Jordan's face pinks up.
Unable to talk, he just nods.

good-bye

Natalie shrugs. Her whole body says,
"Whatever."
Her long legs
cast a troll-like shadow
in the nearly noon sun,
and it follows her back
to her designer world.

I can't believe Jordan
is going to ditch me
and our last two hours of summer together.
"Do you want me to run and get your suit?"
I just stare at him,
an elephant in the birdbath.
"What? I know you love to swim."
It wasn't that long ago
our arms and legs were laced
together in the campground pool.
Doesn't he realize she didn't mean *me*?
I'd rather be in the therapies all summer

than in a pool with perfect Natalie.
"Go with her," I spit.
He bolts off the stoop.
"I'll see you in a month!" he calls
as he disappears behind
the stained-glass door.

like this

Too chicken to face Gran or Mom
I spend hours moping
by the creek,
plopping pebbles, then rocks,
and finally a big stone
until hunger pulls on me,
sends me home.
An enormous quiet meets me—
no pump ticking,
pans rattling,
even the birds are
on a short vacation
from the feeders.

I find Granny
crumpled
next to the claw-footed dresser,
her white blouse stained down the front,
left hand curled like a
dried fern leaf.

fresh-turned soil

My fingers icy,
I misdial the number twice
as I kneel next to Granny.
She's breathing—I check—
but her eyes look blank
as fresh-turned soil,
and she can't answer.

Since I'm upset,
the operator understands only
two words: Grandma hurt.
I'm sure seasons have changed
before the man and woman
rush into the bedroom
with their blue gym bag of equipment
and find me curled up with Granny,
my arm wrapped around her,
and her back soaked
in my tears.

the old lies

They buckle me in the front
with the driver.
Over the screaming siren
she calmly explains—
patting my knee with one hand,
driving with the other—
that they're doing their best for Gran,
but not the old lies
I think I'd rather hear:
that everything will be just fine.

bald, bent old man

The ER social worker is busy handling
a shaken-baby case
(you can overhear everything in an ER),
so they hand me over
to the hospital chaplain.
I'm expecting some bald, bent old man.
Instead,
a woman about Mom's age
rolls up in a sporty wheelchair.
Pastor Anne is patient enough to get
all the answers I know to all the questions
for all of the forms.
She hunts Mom down at Aunt Laura's house,
tells her the story,
and keeps me company—
chatting about movies and Jesus and books,
busy enough to forget my insides have turned
to pudding
for the hours it takes
until Mom arrives
from the city.

two sets of doors

We wait outside the doors
to the intensive-care unit.
Mom lies like it's an old habit—
telling the nurses I'm the required
fourteen years of age—
and a python of guilt squeezes my heart
when I think of the lies I've told
to this point.

They buzz us through two sets of doors.
Before we can go see Gran,
we wash our hands with
a caustic sour soap
and promise not to stay too long.

Mom sucks in her breath when she sees Gran
hooked up to three different bags of solution
drip,
drip,
dripping
into her arm.

Tubes wrap around her face
and up her nose;
the green machine that attaches to it
makes a *whuff, whuff* sound
as it moves.
Her heartbeat bleeps on the monitor,
a soft, slow rhythm.
Mom asks Gran's nurse a blue-million
questions, taking notes and names.
She'll have read the same articles
on stroke recovery by ten tonight—
and she'll talk the talk like a veteran nurse.

But me, I hold Gran's curled hand
and let my silent tears
drip like the IV.

today's special: guilt

Mom sends me to the cafeteria
to get some food and bring back coffee.
I stand in the line,
choose a bagel,
an apple juice with a tinfoil top.
Everything is prepackaged, wrapped
in plastic.
It's not that different from school:
doctors sit together,
and nurses,
and the cafeteria and sanitation workers
wear hairnets.

I shrink into a corner.
The wallpaper, the chairs,
even the landscapes
share the same teal color,
so it's hard to pretend interest.

My thoughts splintered
and my insides shattered
as broken glass.
Gran.

blurt

I must've lost track of time,
because Mom appears in the cafeteria.
When she asks me what happened
I blurt:
"I've been skipping the clinic all week."
My hand covers my mouth.
I didn't mean for that to come out first—
more like last,
or better yet,
never.
Fire crawls up her face;
she stands with her tray and
just a little past loud she says,
"You what?"
And the hospital hushes;
some doctors turn and stare,
the hairnets freeze in their seats,
looking for invisible insects on walls.
She swallows,
sits down.

Her face matches her hair.
In a voice that doesn't seem my own
I answer.
"You didn't bother to *ask* me;
I didn't bother to *tell* you."
She shoots up out of her seat like something bit her.
Crosses her arms, starts to speak but then
walks out.

granny's purse

In the closet at home
hangs Granny's purse—
brown vinyl, almost as big as my backpack.
Ask her for anything,
she usually has it:
paper clip, safety pin, mint,
emery board, lip balm.
It's a walking drugstore.
And seeing it
still hanging on its peg
in the hall closet
and her not home
makes this whole nightmare
real.
While Mom calls her friend, a nurse,
I slip into the closet,
pull the purse from the hook,
and stroke it like it's a small wounded
animal, swallowing sobs.

refusal

In the morning Mom wakes me,
tells me to get ready
for the clinic.
I can't believe she
expects me
to return.

"No."

"What did you say to me?"

"No. I won't go."

"I'll just make you."

"I won't do what they say
even if you do."

She stomps out of my room,
slams my door;

in five minutes, she reappears
with a list of two dozen chores.

"You'll regret it then, Josie.
And don't you even think
about leaving this yard."

After work, she won't even speak
to me.

only the birds

The Morse-code tap of Jordan's knock,
missing.
The hymns Gran hummed,
silent.
The friendly ring of the phone,
mute.
The soap operas Gran pretended not to watch,
outlawed.

Only the birds,
fat on their feeders,
are happy I'm home—
grounded alone.

i miss

I miss
Jordan's
questioning brown eyes,
his curly hair,
his busy building hands.

I miss his
strings of facts,
experiments off track,
long days
just knowing he's there.

tending

Gran's philodendron's arms droop
and mourn;
the tips of the violets are crispy around the edge
as if a match were held there;
the lacy green gloves of tomato plants curl back,
hiding from the sun's angry stare.

Regret,
my only friend,
listens to recordings of my lies
as they play over again in my mind.

Kneeling and tending
I beg the plants:
live
live
live.

empty

The front of the oven looks blank
without Gran's wide frame
stationed there,
and the flower blooms seem to mock her
absence;
the lace of the hammock curled
like a chrysalis
waits for her return.

Jordan's experiments
in his three-square plot
lie abandoned,
forgotten,
left behind like me.

For the first time I feel
as broken inside
as everyone must see
on the outside.

choked by kudzu

There's this vine
called kudzu
someone brought over from
Japan,
trying to make
here
look more like
there.

Thing is,
that vine goes
crazy in this climate,
blanketing whole forests.
No sunlight
or even fresh air
can get under the umbrella
of its leaves
so things can breathe
and grow.

The way Mom and I don't talk
out what happened
grows between us
until the air
feels
choked
like
those
trees.

awake

After Mom's long day at the nursery
we head to the ICU,
stuffing our faces with fast food on the way,
which covers up the not talking—nearly.
After three long days,
just when hope
starts to fade,
Gran's eyes flutter.
She squeezes the doctor's hand
and pulls the tubes
out of her nose,
but she looks so confused
when what she tries to say
comes out like a mouthful of marshmallows.
The worry lines etched
around Mom's eyes fade,
and across the tubes
and the high metal bed
our eyes meet
for just a flash
and a smile.

full of lies

A letter from Jordan:
it's filled with details
about experiments with liquid nitrogen,
helium, and bases.
About a half-dozen kids' names
litter the letter.
I decide not to tell him
about Gran—
not because
I'm a good friend
and don't want to ruin his summer,
'cause I kind of do.
I write replies I'll never send—
about a new neighbor who loves
insects,
the science festival downtown,
weekends spent camping
with Mom and Gran in the mountains—
all lies
about the summer I wish
I was having.

changes

The chores
Mom leaves each day
as punishment
have me falling asleep
almost after dinner:

weeding the gardens,
watering them too,
washing and scrubbing
under sinks, between tiles,
behind the refrigerator.
So when a cramp knocks
between my hip bones
again and again,
I'm sure it's from the work.

Instead I'm surprised to find
my first blood stain.

I stand
on my bed, in just my panties,
to see myself full on in the mirror
and my hands follow curves
where once there were none.

visiting hours

At Lazy Acres I slip back into
old routines:
painting Mrs. Courtney's
yellowing fingernails shell pink,
brushing Miss Ollie's thinning
white hair.
Then Mr. Jakobs and I
sort out his baseball cards
by team and year.

I wheel Gran
down to rehabilitation—
those old tormentors of my own.
A cruel knot tied around my throat
to see her a patient here
instead of serving
her old friends.

small gifts

All morning I gather
every container
I can find—
vases, buckets, even large cups
from the convenience store.

I fill them with cool water from the hose.
I use both my hands, which ache
from the exercise, but I still manage
to cut every stem
of every bloom in the garden:
roses,
asters,
bee balm,
iris,
lilies,
Russian sage,
bachelor's buttons,
coneflower,
coral bells.

Mom's eyes well up when she sees
what I've done, but she still won't cry.
She coughs, blinks, and starts loading
the Jeep full.
Tonight
Gran will sleep
in her garden.

a body can't afford

Our old red Formica kitchen table
stands guard
out by the mailbox
each summer.
It's usually loaded with our crop
of tomatoes
cucumbers, sweet corn, squash,
a scale sheltered
by a Tupperware lid,
plus my faded pink piggy bank.

Granny says
it's an honor system.
She's not one of those old people
who expects the worst
and sees it.
Nope, she hopes for the best
and usually gets it.
Besides, she always says,
if a body can't afford the thirty-five cents

a pound,
they probably need the vegetables
more than we need the coins
for our dishwasher fund.

I watch people slow down,
looking for the table of Gran's organic bounty,
but the vegetables Gran's hands produced
this year we won't share.

paroled

Paroled.

It takes me hours,
but I finally write,
tell Jordan about Gran,
and close with hopes
that he has a good final week
and mean it—
like a real friend
would.

like sun

Gran's coming home! Home!
It feels like the first butterfly
or the golden notes of cardinals
or a whole bed of poppies ablaze.

We can bring her home.
Mom needs to drop off a design
at the nursery. Her office,
not much bigger than a closet,
but I'm impressed to see her name on the door
with manager and designer under it.
It's all she wanted for those
years of school and waiting tables.
On the corner of her messy desk
a photo of me, a baby.
I pick it up, stare,
trying to find myself in
the drooling grin.

Mom plucks it, says:
"I really need a new picture."
Then she looks me
straight in the eye for the first time
since she grounded me and says:
"I know you're not a baby anymore."

"How would you know?
I acted just like one.
I'm sorry, Mom."

"I'm sorry too, Josie-bug." I roll
my eyes at her silly nickname.

I promise Mom I'll exercise and
wear my brace more, but
squeezing my courage, I add:
"But I don't want to take
speech or OT at school anymore."

She sorts papers silently. Finally answers:
"All right, Josie, but I'm hiring a private tutor
for one day after school."

That's fair, I guess.
"But then no more flash card sessions.
I'll study by myself. Deal?"

Mom agrees and then tells me
about a plan for Edna to
come stay with Gran
one night a week so I can work
at the nursery with her.
Just the two of us.
And she asks me what I think.

"I'd like that, Mom."
She pulls me to her
and I feel that old kudzu vine
ripped away between us
and the truth
like sun on my face.

everything looks greener

Summer's nearly over,
but Granny's home,
dragging her left foot,
her left hand
more useless than mine,
dangling by her hip.
Even her left eye and lip
look wilted.
Words crumble
in her mouth
before she can speak them.

Winded
just watering
the house plants,
she sits:
on the benches,
at the kitchen table,
across the daybed,
on the covered porch

that has never held her shadow
very long.

She's home though,
and everything looks
greener with her in it.

soap and syrup

The Morse-code knock on
the old screen door
means
Jordan's home from four weeks at camp.
He's taller, broader, and tanner,
but when he smiles,
my friend appears.
When I show him
Granny's sleeping form
on the old chintz daybed
his face collapses,
tears bloom;
he swallows over and again.
I grab his shoulder,
not letting him turn away.
I kiss his cheek,
then hug him.
He smells like soap and syrup.
A long time
we hold on
to each other.

fall

The winds will blow their own freshness into you, and the storms their energy, while cares will drop away from you like the leaves of autumn.

—John Muir

back to the bus

On the first day
back to school
Mom and Gran make
Jordan and me
a special breakfast.

Mom flips the pancakes
and sausages at the stove,
while Gran stirs the batter
with her good hand,
though she nearly falls asleep
at the table while we eat them.

On the bus,
Natalie Jackson
walks past our mid-bus seat
without so much as a glance.

"I see the real Natalie is back."

"Oh, she never left," he says.
"You remember that day
at her pool? She only wanted me
to fetch the ball for them
when it bounced out.
I didn't even swim."

"Then I guess you're stuck with me, Jordan."

"That's just fine with me."

like cactus

This fall
Mom works most nights
so she can be with Gran
during the days,
which are measured in
doctor's appointments
and daily therapies.

Jordan and I
take turns reading to her
by lamplight.
I show her how to use
my loop scissors
with her wrong/right hand
to cut
the pictures out
of her seed catalogs.

We even teach her
Morse code so she can knock
for what she means to say.

But Granny's sharp words
like cactus needles
have been plucked,
and I miss her
pointed opinions each day.

ping

I never thought
I would ever miss
the sound of
Granny and Mom
exchanging words
like darts.

Now Mom is so
gentle, cautious,
kneeling by her side,
showing her the color
overlays for her first
commercial landscape
design.

The comments
Granny would make
if she could
ping around in my head:
move this here.

This shrub needs a mate.
What fandangled thing is this?
But instead
she just nods,
smiles with half her face.

I bite my lip not to cry,
but Mom lays her head
like a little girl in Gran's lap
and lets the tears
stain her ancient
mint robe
at last.

double bubblegum blooms

Gran's friend Edna
(the one who stays too long
but brings the best carrot cake
so we suffer her latest complaints,
nodding through mouthfuls),
brought Gran another sick patient.
An African violet
with crown rot—
pitiful swollen stems
that drop if you
breathe too hard on them;
heart-shaped leaves
hanging their heads
like a kid who just got scolded.

It took some time
for her damaged hands to nurse it back,
but finally
double bubblegum-colored blooms
reflect in the frosted window
above the porcelain sink.

fourteen candles

I bet a lot of kids
wish for the same thing
as I will this year
with my fourteen candles:

for things to be
just like they were.

snort

I'm lugging homework home—
it feels like
an elephant in my backpack.
Homework should be outlawed
on birthdays—
even ones nobody mentions all day.
I nearly fall through the door
to find
Granny at the kitchen table
pointing
and nodding.
By the look on her face
she might cuss if she could.
Burnt sausage in her iron skillet
and Jordan dusted in flour,
trying to roll out dough.

They both look up—
caught
trying to make my
birthday favorite:

breakfast for dinner,
Granny's biscuits and gravy
on the red plate!

Out of nowhere
Granny flings her good arm—
a dollop of dough
sticks for just a second to Jordan's forehead.
She snorts behind her hand.
Then he lobs a glob
of unbaked biscuit at me—
soon the kitchen is covered
in flour,
biscuit balls,
and laughter.

first

Jordan and I
keep laughing
over Mom's surprised face
when she walks in on our flour fight
and then joins in.
It's a day
we both don't want
to end, standing
near the door on the screened porch,
though neither of us
reaches to open it
first.

On impulse I say,
"Wait here."
I give him the journal of letters
about my imaginary summer.
I know he'll understand it.
When I slip it in his hands,
I realize

he's shot up taller than me
and so fast that later I question
whether it really happened at all—
one quick kiss—
then he nearly falls
rushing out the door.
The wind stinging my face
as I watch his dark figure escaping
into the lavender glow of the night.

dreams

What do you want to be?
adults always ask,
as if you know
by fourteen
what you want to be doing
at forty-five.
I used to make up stuff:
firewoman,
pediatrician,
astronaut,
all the people
I knew my mom
wanted to hear.

I know
more what I don't want to be:
a single parent,
poor,
stuck behind some desk
or in school longer than
I need to go.

And that will have to be
enough

for now.

eiffel tower

I decide to finish
the Eiffel Tower mural on the old shed
as a Christmas gift for Gran.
It may take this whole season, but I've learned
if I take my time, nothing can stop me.
My fingers sweat inside the rawhide gloves,
the tools for glasswork awkward in my hands.
But I make a little progress each day.
Mom has taken to standing below the stepladder,
shading her eyes with her hand,
talking to my back as I work.
I step down to get a wider view.
"I'm going there someday, you know."
I say it out of nowhere, but realize I mean it.
"I believe you," she whispers.
"You do?"
Mom's cool fingers tilt my chin up at her.
"I believe *in* you, Josie."
And I press her words
in the pages of my heart
like a first spring bloom.

hammock

Shoe to shoe,
leg to leg,
arm to arm,
familiar fingers,
Jordan and I
sway in the hammock
on the autumn breeze.

I convince Jordan we should
join the Young Scientists Club
together
so we can go on their annual trip
to the Smithsonian museums
in the spring.

The pale sky and changing leaves
create a kaleidoscope of color
tumbling and fluttering
around our new plans
and dreams.

better than my own

It's the last chance to plant bulbs
for spring,
so I drag a chair
from patch to patch.
Gran shuffles to
her spot and gives me clear
directions with a series
of grunts, nods, gestures.

I understand her wishes
better than my own.

I unroll a length of
yarn
that has laid
dusty far too long
this summer.

Tears puddle in her eyes
and her smile wobbles

as she sees I've
spelled her name
with daffodils:
Jocelyn

reaching

Even after summer
packs her bags,
the garden blooms:
holly drips berries
for the birds;
the river birch
peels back
to show its pale heart.

A museum opening
of frozen sculpture:
Japanese maple limbs
painted with fresh frost,
ornamental grasses
pause time.

And me,
I'm the wisteria vine
growing up the arbor of this
odd family,
reaching for sun.

Acknowledgments

This book grew over many seasons with the generous care and insights from many friends: Sue Corbett, Diane M. Davis, Susan Greene, Kim Marcus, Lynne Pisano, Andria Rosenblum, Deb Svenson, Kyra Teis, and support at The Pub. My twin, Trish DeLong, who gossips with me about my characters as if they live down the block, and my mom, who listens to poems over the phone. The divine duo: Jessica Swaim and Julia Durango, who held my hand through every page of every draft. My agent, Barry Goldblatt, for his unwavering faith. Melanie Cecka, who pulled the ribbon of the story from my clenched palm, and the entire Bloomsbury crew for their boundless creativity and enthusiasm. The real Aunt Laura Collier, for everlasting friendship. Thanks, always and always, to my husband, Randy, for believing. And for Cole and Abbie, who inspire every word.